A Season With
Wally The Green Monster ™

Jerry Remy

Illustrated by Kevin Coffey

MASCOT BOOKS
www.mascotbooks.com

It had been a long, cold winter in New England. *Wally The Green Monster,* the world-famous mascot of the *Boston Red Sox,* was enjoying his winter vacation.

After baseball season, Wally turned his attention to some of his favorite cold-weather activities. Wally especially loved to go ice fishing and snowmobiling. On Groundhog Day, Wally watched as Punxsutawney Phil saw his shadow. There would be another six weeks of winter!

Fortunately for Wally, he was heading to warm, sunny Florida for Red Sox Spring Training again, and the start of a new baseball season.

Wally The Green Monster packed his bags and drove to Logan Airport. He boarded an airplane and took his seat in the First Class section. The flight attendants were happy to see their favorite mascot. They said, "Hello, Wally!"

The airplane zoomed down the runway and
headed south toward Fort Myers, Florida –
the Spring Training home of the Boston Red
Sox. As Wally exited the plane, he was surprised
to see so many Red Sox fans awaiting his
arrival. The fans cheered, "Hello, Wally!"

Wanting to soak up the Florida sunshine, Wally's first stop was beautiful Fort Myers Beach. Wally built a sand castle model of his favorite ballpark. A Red Sox fan spotted the mascot and called, "Hello, Wally!"

After spending several hours on the beach, it was time for Wally to report to City of Palms Park, where he received his uniform and baseball equipment. Excited to see the team's mascot, the players said, "Hello, Wally!"

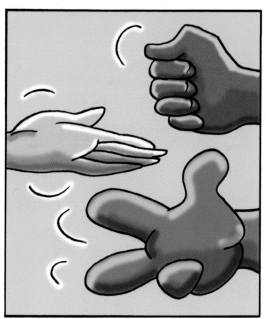

At Spring Training, Wally and the entire
Boston Red Sox team practiced important
baseball skills, like batting, bunting, fielding,
and base running. There was also time
for some fun, too.

Wally played *Rock, Paper, Scissors* with his teammates. He also organized a bubblegum blowing contest, which he won!

Wally's favorite part of Spring Training was visiting with the many Red Sox fans who had traveled from all over the world to see their beloved team. As Wally rode a golf cart around the ballpark, fans called, "Hello, Wally!"

As the calendar turned to March, the Red Sox played Spring Training games in the Grapefruit League. On St. Patrick's Day, the team wore special green jerseys. Not wanting to get pinched, Wally also wore a green jersey.

Meanwhile, back in Boston, New Englanders celebrated the special holiday by attending parades throughout the city.

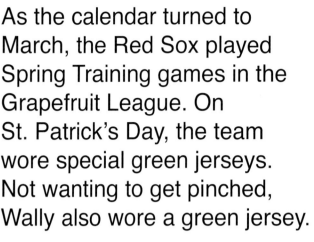

The Red Sox returned to Boston the first week in April for the start of the season. On Opening Day, Red Sox fans bundled up and made their way to historic Fenway Park. Everyone was excited that it was baseball time again.

As each player's name was called, they ran from the Red Sox dugout to the first base line. The players removed their caps and gazed at the American Flag for the singing of the National Anthem.

"Play Ball!" called the umpire. The season had begun!

As spring turned to summer, the weather warmed
and the Boston Red Sox played great baseball.
On Independence Day, the team was leading the
American League East Division and *Red Sox
Nation* was happy. Following an afternoon game
at Fenway Park on the Fourth of July,

Wally and Red Sox fans celebrated the holiday by attending the annual Boston Pops Orchestra concert at Hatch Shell near the Charles River. While patriotic music played, colorful fireworks exploded in the night sky. Wally was proud to be an American!

In September, the baseball season was winding down. Thanks to more great play, the Red Sox won the American League East Division. September also marked back-to-school time all over Red Sox Nation.

Wally, two Red Sox players, and Jerry Remy, drove to a nearby school for a special visit. Jerry read one of his famous Wally The Green Monster books to the children. The students cheered, "Hello, RemDawg!"

October meant it was time for the *Major League Baseball* playoffs. The Red Sox first played in a best-of-five Division Series, which they won. The American League Championship Series was next, with the winner advancing to the *World Series*.

The Red Sox played hard and won the ALCS.
They were going to another World Series!
Players and fans cheered, "Let's go, Red Sox!"

In the World Series, the Red Sox played the
National League Champions in a best-of-seven
series. Fans all over Red Sox Nation watched
each game and cheered for their team.
With great hitting, pitching and defense, the
Red Sox won the World Series!

The Boston Red Sox were World Series Champions again! Wally joined his teammates on the field following the last out. The players gave each other hugs and high fives.

The players cheered, "We did it, Wally! We're World Series Champions!"

After the championship season, it was time to honor the Red Sox with a parade. Red Sox fans braved the cold November air and lined the streets of Boston to cheer the team's accomplishments. Fans from near and far came out to greet their local heroes.

Wally and the players tipped their caps to fans and thanked them for their loyal support.
Red Sox fans cheered for their favorite players and their favorite mascot. Everyone in Red Sox Nation was happy!

After another eventful season, Wally was
happy to spend the winter months resting
quietly in his cozy home at Fenway Park. In
front of a warm fire, Wally sat in his Adirondack
chair and thought about how much fun it was
being the mascot for the World Series
Champions Boston Red Sox.

Good night, Wally.

To my favorite Wally fan, my grandson, Dominik. ~ Jerry Remy

For my nephew Jonathon. ~ Kevin Coffey

For more information about our products,
please visit us online at www.mascotbooks.com.

Mascot Books, Inc.
P.O. Box 220157
Chantilly, VA 20153-0157

Major League Baseball trademarks and copyrights are used
with permission of Major League Baseball Properties, Inc.

ISBN: 978-1-934878-07-1

Printed in the United States.

www.mascotbooks.com

www.mascotbooks.com

Title List

Baseball

Boston Red Sox	Hello, *Wally*!	Jerry Remy
Boston Red Sox	*Wally The Green Monster And His Journey Through Red Sox Nation*!	Jerry Remy
Boston Red Sox	Coast to Coast with *Wally The Green Monster*	Jerry Remy
Boston Red Sox	A Season with *Wally The Green Monster*	Jerry Remy
Colorado Rockies	Hello, *Dinger*!	Aimee Aryal
Detroit Tigers	Hello, *Paws*!	Aimee Aryal
New York Yankees	Let's Go, *Yankees*!	Yogi Berra
New York Yankees	*Yankees* Town	Aimee Aryal
New York Mets	Hello, *Mr. Met*!	Rusty Staub
New York Mets	*Mr. Met* and his Journey Through the Big Apple	Aimee Aryal
St. Louis Cardinals	Hello, *Fredbird*!	Ozzie Smith
Philadelphia Phillies	Hello, *Phillie Phanatic*!	Aimee Aryal
Chicago Cubs	Let's Go, *Cubs*!	Aimee Aryal
Chicago White Sox	Let's Go, *White Sox*!	Aimee Aryal
Cleveland Indians	Hello, *Slider*!	Bob Feller
Seattle Mariners	Hello, *Mariner Moose*!	Aimee Aryal
Washington Nationals	Hello, *Screech*!	Aimee Aryal
Milwaukee Brewers	Hello, *Bernie Brewer*!	Aimee Aryal

College

Alabama	Hello, Big Al!	Aimee Aryal
Alabama	Roll Tide!	Ken Stabler
Alabama	Big Al's Journey Through the Yellowhammer State	Aimee Aryal
Arizona	Hello, Wilbur!	Lute Olson
Arkansas	Hello, Big Red!	Aimee Aryal
Arkansas	Big Red's Journey Through the Razorback State	Aimee Aryal
Auburn	Hello, Aubie!	Aimee Aryal
Auburn	War Eagle!	Pat Dye
Auburn	Aubie's Journey Through the Yellowhammer State	Aimee Aryal
Boston College	Hello, Baldwin!	Aimee Aryal
Brigham Young	Hello, Cosmo!	LaVell Edwards
Cal - Berkeley	Hello, Oski!	Aimee Aryal
Clemson	Hello, Tiger!	Aimee Aryal
Clemson	Tiger's Journey Through the Palmetto State	Aimee Aryal
Colorado	Hello, Ralphie!	Aimee Aryal
Connecticut	Hello, Jonathan!	Aimee Aryal
Duke	Hello, Blue Devil!	Aimee Aryal
Florida	Hello, Albert!	Aimee Aryal
Florida	Albert's Journey Through the Sunshine State	Aimee Aryal
Florida State	Let's Go, 'Noles!	Aimee Aryal
Georgia	Hello, Hairy Dawg!	Aimee Aryal
Georgia	How 'Bout Them Dawgs!	Vince Dooley
Georgia	Hairy Dawg's Journey Through the Peach State	Vince Dooley
Georgia Tech	Hello, Buzz!	Aimee Aryal
Gonzaga	Spike, The Gonzaga Bulldog	Mike Pringle
Illinois	Let's Go, Illini!	Aimee Aryal
Indiana	Let's Go, Hoosiers!	Aimee Aryal
Iowa	Hello, Herky!	Aimee Aryal
Iowa State	Hello, Cy!	Amy DeLashmutt
James Madison	Hello, Duke Dog!	Aimee Aryal
Kansas	Hello, Big Jay!	Aimee Aryal
Kansas State	Hello, Willie!	Dan Walter
Kentucky	Hello, Wildcat!	Aimee Aryal
LSU	Hello, Mike!	Aimee Aryal
LSU	Mike's Journey Through the Bayou State	Aimee Aryal
Maryland	Hello, Testudo!	Aimee Aryal
Michigan	Let's Go, Blue!	Aimee Aryal
Michigan State	Hello, Sparty!	Aimee Aryal
Minnesota	Hello, Goldy!	Aimee Aryal
Mississippi	Hello, Colonel Rebel!	Aimee Aryal

Pro Football

Carolina Panthers	Let's Go, Panthers!	Aimee Aryal
Chicago Bears	Let's Go, Bears!	Aimee Aryal
Dallas Cowboys	How 'Bout Them Cowboys!	Aimee Aryal
Green Bay Packers	Go, Pack, Go!	Aimee Aryal
Kansas City Chiefs	Let's Go, Chiefs!	Aimee Aryal
Minnesota Vikings	Let's Go, Vikings!	Aimee Aryal
New York Giants	Let's Go, Giants!	Aimee Aryal
New York Jets	J-E-T-S! Jets, Jets, Jets!	Aimee Aryal
New England Patriots	Let's Go, Patriots!	Aimee Aryal
Seattle Seahawks	Let's Go, Seahawks!	Aimee Aryal
Washington Redskins	Hail To The Redskins!	Aimee Aryal

Basketball

Dallas Mavericks	Let's Go, Mavs!	Mark Cuban
Boston Celtics	Let's Go, Celtics!	Aimee Aryal

Other

Kentucky Derby	White Diamond Runs For The Roses	Aimee Aryal
Marine Corps Marathon	Run, Miles, Run!	Aimee Aryal
Mississippi State	Hello, Bully!	Aimee Aryal
Missouri	Hello, Truman!	Todd Donoho
Nebraska	Hello, Herbie Husker!	Aimee Aryal
North Carolina	Hello, Rameses!	Aimee Aryal
North Carolina	Rameses' Journey Through the Tar Heel State	Aimee Aryal
North Carolina St.	Hello, Mr. Wuf!	Aimee Aryal
North Carolina St.	Mr. Wuf's Journey Through North Carolina	Aimee Aryal
Notre Dame	Let's Go, Irish!	Aimee Aryal
Ohio State	Hello, Brutus!	Aimee Aryal
Ohio State	Brutus' Journey	Aimee Aryal
Oklahoma	Let's Go, Sooners!	Aimee Aryal
Oklahoma State	Hello, Pistol Pete!	Aimee Aryal
Oregon	Go Ducks!	Aimee Aryal
Oregon State	Hello, Benny the Beaver!	Aimee Aryal
Penn State	Hello, Nittany Lion!	Aimee Aryal
Penn State	We Are Penn State!	Joe Paterno
Purdue	Hello, Purdue Pete!	Aimee Aryal
Rutgers	Hello, Scarlet Knight!	Aimee Aryal
South Carolina	Hello, Cocky!	Aimee Aryal
South Carolina	Cocky's Journey Through the Palmetto State	Aimee Aryal
So. California	Hello, Tommy Trojan!	Aimee Aryal
Syracuse	Hello, Otto!	Aimee Aryal
Tennessee	Hello, Smokey!	Aimee Aryal
Tennessee	Smokey's Journey Through the Volunteer State	Aimee Aryal
Texas	Hello, Hook 'Em!	Aimee Aryal
Texas	Hook 'Em's Journey Through the Lone Star State	Aimee Aryal
Texas A & M	Howdy, Reveille!	Aimee Aryal
Texas A & M	Reveille's Journey Through the Lone Star State	Aimee Aryal
Texas Tech	Hello, Masked Rider!	Aimee Aryal
UCLA	Hello, Joe Bruin!	Aimee Aryal
Virginia	Hello, CavMan!	Aimee Aryal
Virginia Tech	Hello, Hokie Bird!	Aimee Aryal
Virginia Tech	Yea, It's Hokie Game Day!	Frank Beamer
Virginia Tech	Hokie Bird's Journey Through Virginia	Aimee Aryal
Wake Forest	Hello, Demon Deacon!	Aimee Aryal
Washington	Hello, Harry the Husky!	Aimee Aryal
Washington State	Hello, Butch!	Aimee Aryal
West Virginia	Hello, Mountaineer!	Aimee Aryal
Wisconsin	Hello, Bucky!	Aimee Aryal
Wisconsin	Bucky's Journey Through the Badger State	Aimee Aryal